I0712757

Copyright © 2024 by Shaleea Venney

All rights reserved. No part of this publication may be reproduced, stored, or transmitted in any form or by any means, electronic, mechanical, photocopying, recording, scanning, or otherwise without written permission from the publisher. It is illegal to copy this book, post it to a website, or distribute it by any other means without permission.

Shaleea Venney asserts the moral right to be identified as the author of this work.

To the person planning their departure:
This book is not something you wanted but it's good
you have it now because it was created to help you.
Take a deep breath, sit in your thoughts, and speak
your truth from the heart. Someone in your life needs
this from you and will treasure it. This is your final
act of love. Make it count.

To the Grieving Recipient:
Your loved one left this for you because they wanted
you to keep them close in your heart. They are with
you forever. Carry them in your spirit and when you
miss them, come back to them through this book. It's
gonna be OK.

AFTER
WE SAY
GOODBYE
The Partner's Edition

A Keepsake Book from:

TYPE:MORTUARY /FUNERAL PLANNING	NAME:		ACCOUNT NUMBER:
CONTACT INFO:	LOCATION:	VALUE:	DATE:

TYPE: HOSPICE AGENCY	NAME:		ACCOUNT NUMBER:
CONTACT INFO:	LOCATION :	VALUE:	DATE:

TYPE: LIFE INSURANCE/ INSURANCE	NAME:		ACCOUNT NUMBER:
CONTACT INFO:	LOCATION OF INFORMATION:	VALUE:	DATE:

Here are my accounts and passwords

BANK ACCOUNTS

TYPE:	INSTITUTION:		ACCOUNT NO.:
OWNERS OF ACCOUNT:		INSTITUTION CONTACTS INFO:	
STATEMENTS SENT TO (PHYSICAL ADDDRESS OR EMAIL ADDRESS):		AUTOMATED PAYMENT FORM:	
LOCATION OF CHECKS AND USED CHECKBOOKS:	ATM AND DEBIT CARDS FOR ACCOUNT:	ATM PIN:	

TYPE:	INSTITUTION:		ACCOUNT NO.:
OWNERS OF ACCOUNT:		INSTITUTION CONTACTS INFO:	
STATEMENTS SENT TO (PHYSICAL ADDDRESS OR EMAIL ADDRESS):		AUTOMATED PAYMENT FORM:	
LOCATION OF CHECKS AND USED CHECKBOOKS:	ATM AND DEBIT CARDS FOR ACCOUNT:	ATM PIN:	

TYPE:	INSTITUTION:		ACCOUNT NO.:
OWNERS OF ACCOUNT:		INSTITUTION CONTACTS INFO:	
STATEMENTS SENT TO (PHYSICAL ADDDRESS OR EMAIL ADDRESS):		AUTOMATED PAYMENT FORM:	
LOCATION OF CHECKS AND USED CHECKBOOKS:	ATM AND DEBIT CARDS FOR ACCOUNT:	ATM PIN:	

INVESTMENTS

Investments (including mutual funds, amenities and stocks)

WHERE TO FIND:

TYPE:	NAME:		ACCOUNT NUMBER:
CONTACT INFO:	LOCATION OF INFORMATION:	VALUE:	DATE:

TYPE:	NAME:		ACCOUNT NUMBER:
CONTACT INFO:	LOCATION OF INFORMATION:	VALUE:	DATE:

TYPE:	NAME:		ACCOUNT NUMBER:
CONTACT INFO:	LOCATION OF INFORMATION:	VALUE:	DATE:

TYPE:	NAME:		ACCOUNT NUMBER:
CONTACT INFO:	LOCATION OF INFORMATION:	VALUE:	DATE:

RETIREMENT PLANS

Retirement Plans (40k,pensons, TFCA, etc.)

WHERE TO FIND:

TYPE:	NAME:		ACCOUNT NUMBER:
CONTACT INFO:	LOCATION OF INFORMATION:	VALUE:	DATE:

TYPE:	NAME:		ACCOUNT NUMBER:
CONTACT INFO:	LOCATION OF INFORMATION:	VALUE:	DATE:

TYPE:	NAME:		ACCOUNT NUMBER:
CONTACT INFO:	LOCATION OF INFORMATION:	VALUE:	DATE:

TYPE:	NAME:		ACCOUNT NUMBER:
CONTACT INFO:	LOCATION OF INFORMATION:	VALUE:	DATE:

PASSWORD TRACKER

NAME:
EMAIL:
USERNAME:
PASSWORD:
NOTES:

NAME:
EMAIL:
USERNAME:
PASSWORD:
NOTES:

NAME:
EMAIL:
USERNAME:
PASSWORD:
NOTES:

NAME:
EMAIL:
USERNAME:
PASSWORD:
NOTES:

NAME:
EMAIL:
USERNAME:
PASSWORD:
NOTES:

NAME:
EMAIL:
USERNAME:
PASSWORD:
NOTES:

NAME:
EMAIL:
USERNAME:
PASSWORD:
NOTES:

NAME:
EMAIL:
USERNAME:
PASSWORD:
NOTES:

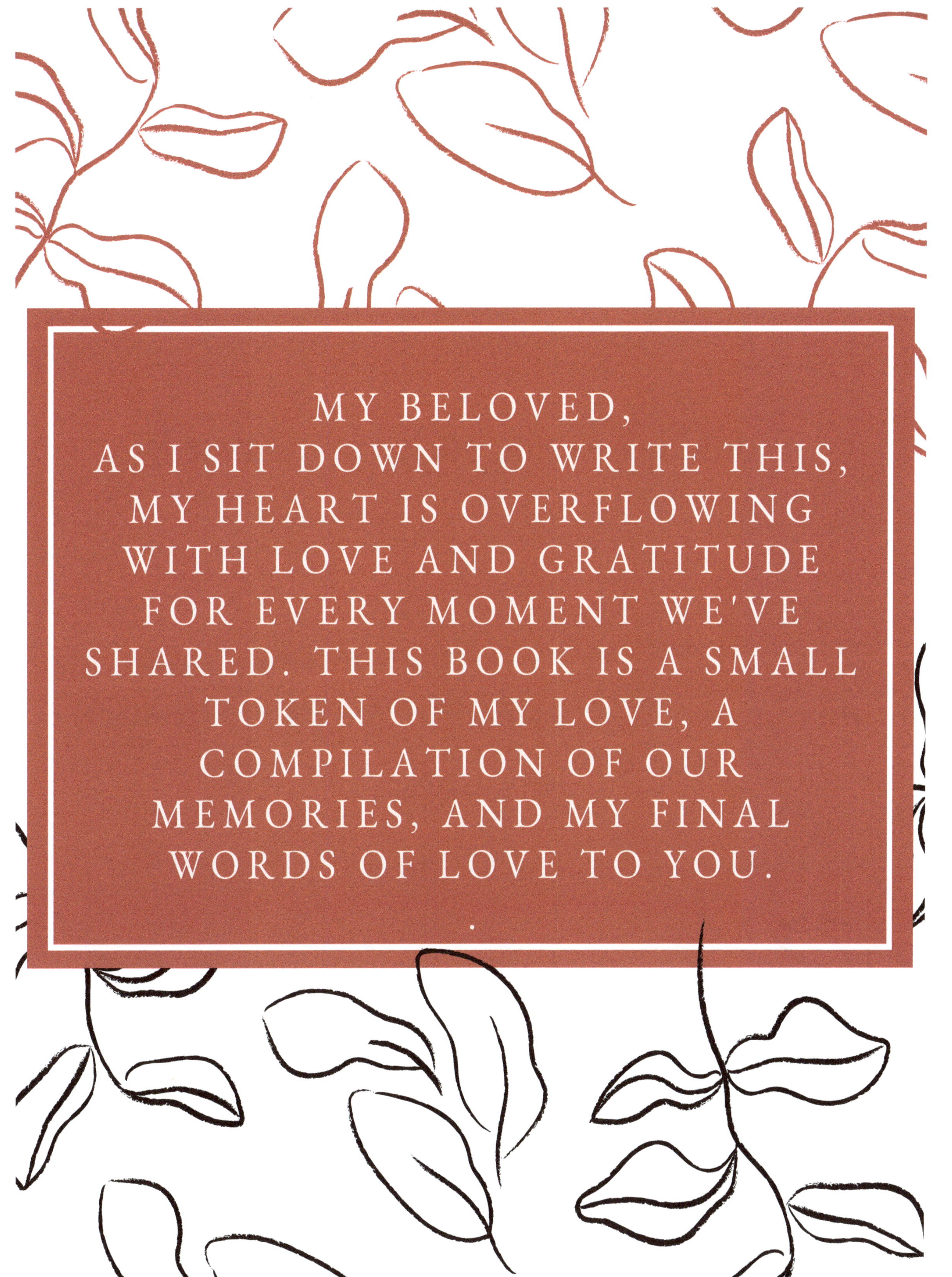

MY BELOVED,
AS I SIT DOWN TO WRITE THIS,
MY HEART IS OVERFLOWING
WITH LOVE AND GRATITUDE
FOR EVERY MOMENT WE'VE
SHARED. THIS BOOK IS A SMALL
TOKEN OF MY LOVE, A
COMPILATION OF OUR
MEMORIES, AND MY FINAL
WORDS OF LOVE TO YOU.

Would I like to be buried or cremated?

If cremated, here's what I'd like you to do with my ashes:

To my sweetheart,

In you, I found my love, my partner, and my best friend. This book is a celebration of our journey together.♥

When it hits you that I am really gone remember this...

SECTION 1:
HOW WE BEGAN

- OUR FIRST MEETING: HOW IT FELT AND WHAT DREW ME TO YOU.
- EARLY DAYS OF OUR RELATIONSHIP: FAVORITE DATES AND PIVOTAL MOMENTS.
- THE DAY WE GOT MARRIED/COMMITTED TO EACH OTHER: MY FEELINGS AND PROMISES.

Notes

date:

Notes

date:

Notes

date:

Notes

date:

Notes

date:

Notes

date:

Notes

date:

ON THE HARD DAYS
REMEMBER:

• I AM FOREVER WITH YOU
• I LOVE YOUR SMILE AND
DON'T WANT YOU TO BE
SAD
• YOU CAN TALK TO ME. YOU
MIGHT NOT HEAR MY
VOICE BUT DEEP DOWN
YOU KNOW WHAT I WOULD
SAY

SECTION 2:
OUR BEST MOMENTS
TOGETHER

• ADVENTURES AND TRAVELS
WE EMBARKED ON.
• CHALLENGES WE OVERCAME
AS A TEAM.
• SMALL, EVERYDAY MOMENTS
THAT MEANT THE WORLD TO
ME.

Notes

date:

Notes

date:

Notes

date:

Notes

date:

Notes

date:

Notes

date:

Notes

date:

IT WAS ALWAYS YOU!

- I HAVE LOVED YOU SINCE THE DAY WE MET
- YOU ARE THE BEST PART OF ME, THE LOVE OF MY LIFE!
- I AM SO PROUD OF THE LOVE WE SHARED! MY LIFE WAS BETTER BECAUSE OF YOUR LOVE.

SECTION 3:
WHAT I ADMIRE
ABOUT YOU

• YOUR QUALITIES THAT I ADORE AND RESPECT.
• TIMES YOU'VE INSPIRED OR SUPPORTED ME.
• THE IMPACT YOU'VE HAD ON MY LIFE.

Notes

date:

Notes

date:

Notes

date:

Notes

date:

Don't Forget to Live Baby!

IT IS OK TO MISS ME BUT LIVE YOUR LIFE. HONOR ME BY DOING WHAT MAKES YOU HAPPY.
DON'T EVER, EVER, MOVE ON! (I AM JUST KIDDING) I WANT YOU TO BE HAPPY!
IF YOU FALL IN LOVE WITH A SWEET SOMEONE, LET IT HAPPEN. BE HAPPY. IT DOESN'T CHANGE OUR LOVE. YOU DESERVE TO LOVE AND BE LOVED.

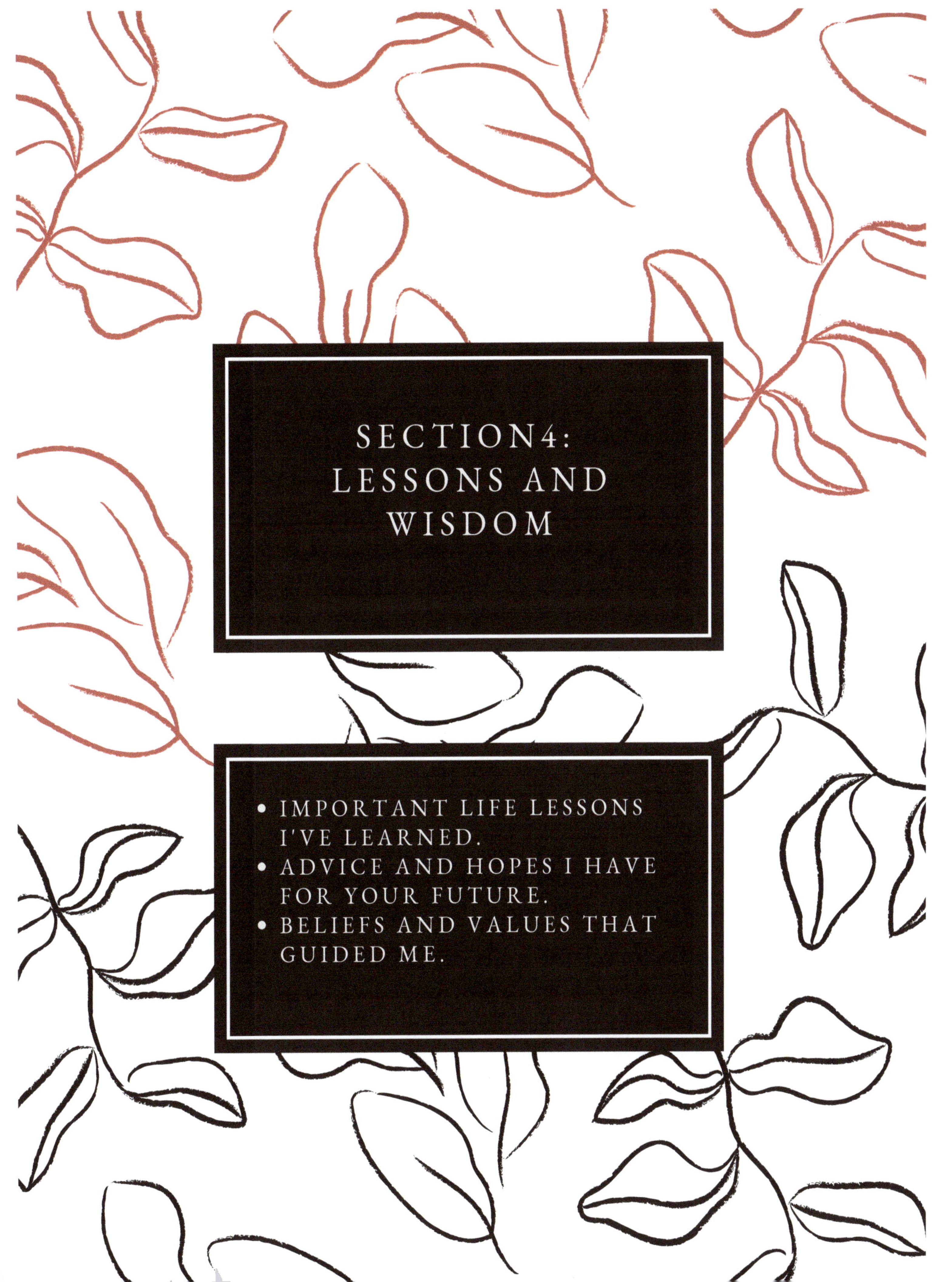
SECTION4:
LESSONS AND
WISDOM

IMPORTANT LIFE LESSONS
I'VE LEARNED.
ADVICE AND HOPES I HAVE
FOR YOUR FUTURE.
BELIEFS AND VALUES THAT
GUIDED ME.

Notes

date:

Notes

date:

Notes

date:

Notes

date:

Notes

date:

KEEP ME WITH YOU!

• IF WE HAVE GRANDBABIES, TELL THEM ABOUT ME AND HOW MUCH I WOULD LOVE THEM.
• KEEP OUR TRADITIONS AND THINK OF ME AND SMILE KNOWING I AM THERE.
• ALWAYS HOLD ON TO MY LOVE FOR YOU!

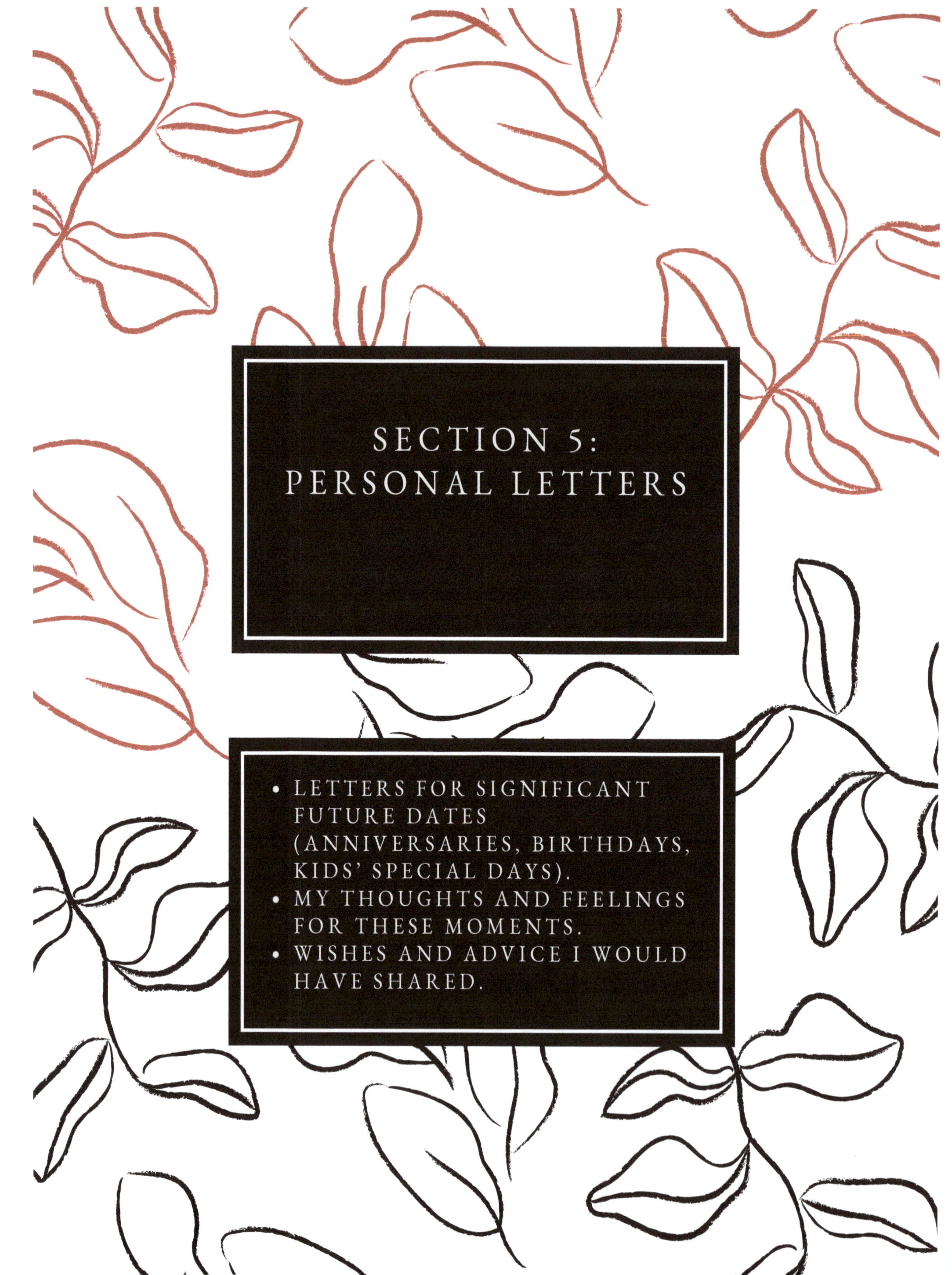

SECTION 5:
PERSONAL LETTERS

- LETTERS FOR SIGNIFICANT FUTURE DATES (ANNIVERSARIES, BIRTHDAYS, KIDS' SPECIAL DAYS).
- MY THOUGHTS AND FEELINGS FOR THESE MOMENTS.
- WISHES AND ADVICE I WOULD HAVE SHARED.

Notes

date:

Notes

date:

Notes

date:

Notes

date:

Notes

date:

Notes

date:

Notes

date:

I WISH WE HAD MORE TIME!

• HOW I WISH I COULD'VE STAYED WITH YOU!
• I HATED HAVING TO LEAVE YOU
• PLEASE FIND PEACE IN THE FACT THAT WE WILL SEE EACH OTHER AGAIN. SEE YOU LATER BABY...

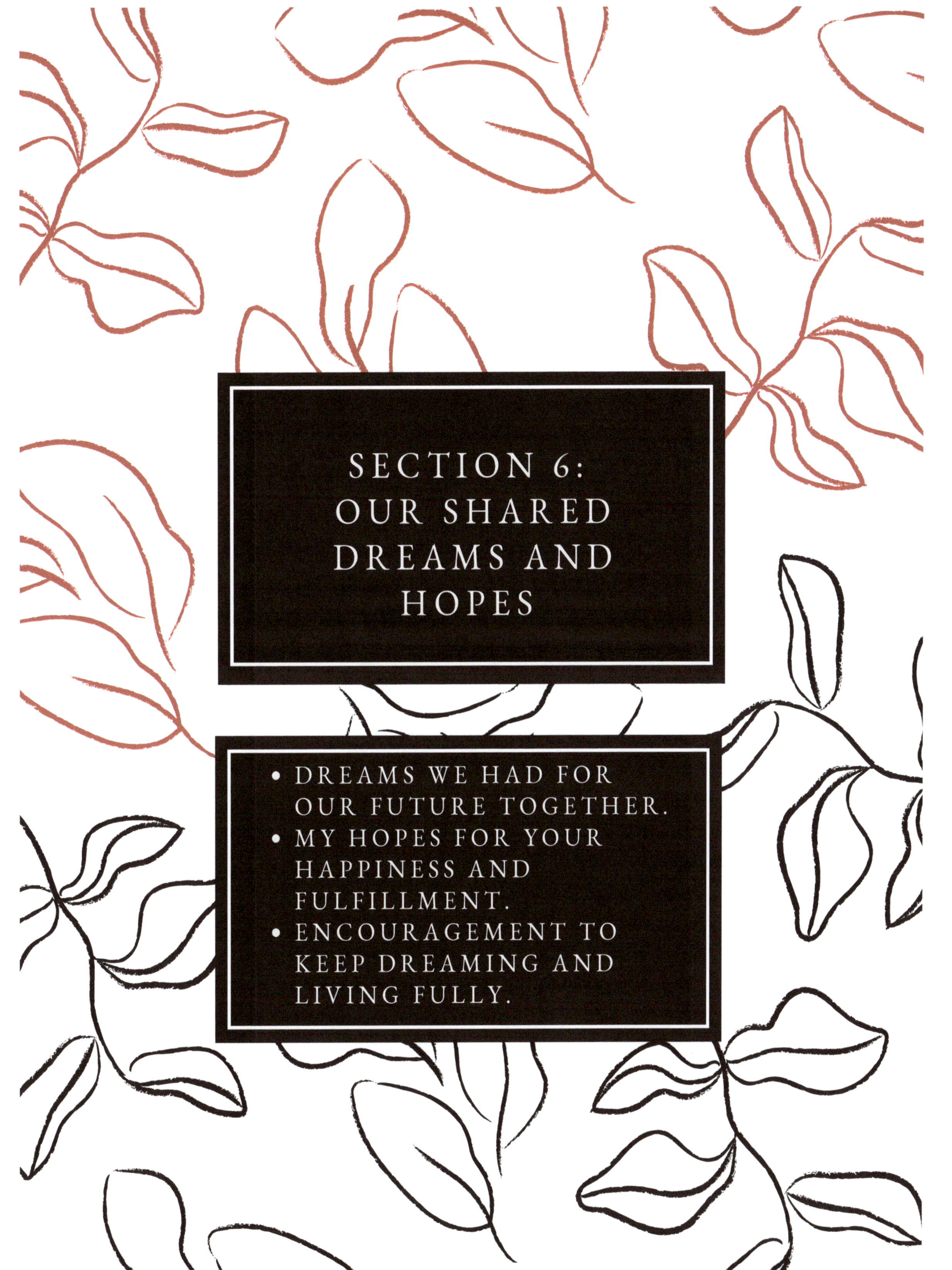

SECTION 6:
OUR SHARED
DREAMS AND
HOPES

DREAMS WE HAD FOR
OUR FUTURE TOGETHER.
MY HOPES FOR YOUR
HAPPINESS AND
FULFILLMENT.
ENCOURAGEMENT TO
KEEP DREAMING AND
LIVING FULLY.

Notes

date:

Notes

date:

Notes

date:

Notes

date:

Notes

Notes

date:

Notes

date:

Notes

date:

Notes

date:

Notes

date:

YOU ARE SO LOVED!

• IN CASE I DIDN'T TELL YOU ENOUGH, I LOVE YOU SO MUCH!
• OUR LOVE STORY IS THE BEST ONE I EVER HEARD.
• I HAVE ALWAYS BEEN IN AWE OF YOU. YOU MADE ME SO PROUD TO CALL YOU MINE. THANKS FOR DOING LIFE WITH ME, IT WAS MY PLEASURE.

SECTION 7:
FINAL LOVE
LETTER

- MY ENDURING LOVE FOR YOU.
- HOW I WISH TO BE REMEMBERED IN YOUR HEART.
- MY FINAL WORDS OF LOVE AND GOODBYE.

Notes

date:

Notes

date:

Notes

date:

Notes

date:

SPACE FOR YOU

HERE I HAVE LEFT SPACE FOR YOU.
- PAGES FOR YOU TO WRITE YOUR OWN MEMORIES OF ME.
- SPACES FOR PHOTOS OR DRAWINGS THAT ARE SPECIAL TO YOU.

Notes

date:

Notes

date:

Notes

date:

Notes

date:

Notes

date:

Photos

Photos

Photos

Photos

Photos

Photos

Photos

Photos

Photos

www.ingramcontent.com/pod-product-compliance
Lightning Source LLC
Chambersburg PA
CBHW041159300726

48981CB00004B/306